# RoCKiN' yOur WoRld

# 'N SYNC

BY DEVRA NEWBERGER SPEREGEN

**SCHOLASTIC INC.**

New York  Toronto  London  Auckland  Sydney
Mexico City  New Delhi  Hong Kong

Photography credits: 'N Sync cover: Bernhard Kuhmstedt/Retna; FIVE
cover: Ilpo Musto/London Features; Page 1: Bernhard Kuhmstedt/Retna;
Pages 2–3: Ilpo Musto/London Features; Page 4: Anthony Cutajar/London
Features; Page 5: Ilpo Musto/London Features; Page 6: Anthony
Cutajar/London Features; Page 8 (top): Anthony Cutajar/London Features;
Page 8 (bottom): Bernhard Kuhmstedt/Retna; Page 9: Dennis Van
Tine/London Features; Page 10 (top): Collin Bell/Retna; Page 10 (bottom):
Justin Thomas/All Action; Pages 11–15: Anthony Cutajar/London
Features; Page 16: Bernhard Kuhmstedt/Retna.

ISBN 0-439-13549-4

12 11 10 9 8 7 6 5 4 3                    9/9 0 1 2 3 4/0

Printed in the U.S.A.                          40

First Scholastic printing, August 1999

# 'N Sync

The music rocks, the band rules, each babe is severely crush-worthy. Is it any wonder 'N Sync is *everything*? And now this, too: For your reading "'n-joyment," an 'N Sync-lo-pedia of facts, favorites, and fun stuff you never knew!

# Chapter 1

# The Boys
# of Summer Tour

Whether you've managed to snag those hard-to-get floor seats for the 'N Sync tour this summer, or whether you're holding tickets for the last row, rest assured you're in for the most thrilling event of your life: 'N Sync's "The Boys of Summer" tour! It doesn't matter who your fave is, or how much of your allowance you spent on the ticket. Once you step through the stadium doors . . . you're in!

"There are no bad seats," according to Lance Bass, one of 'N Sync's hunky, bleached-babes. As he revealed to his adoring fans on-line recently, "We're going to be *really* close to everyone in the arena. You'll have a really good seat . . . wherever you are!"

Leave it to the guys with "the best fans in the world" to make it so easy to check out their tour. Whether it's the massive "Meet and Greet" sessions they hold backstage before each and every concert, or whether it's the lucky few they pull on stage during the show, with 'N Sync what you see is what you get. And what you *get* is a dedicated, passionate bunch of guys whose main concern is for their fans!

Despite the fact that 'N Sync broke records selling out the tour, when it comes to bringing fans their music — a warm, soulful ballad or a kickin' jiggy dance tune — the guys make sure they go all out for number one: *you!* During their last tour, when the guys heard tickets sold out so quickly that thousands of fans couldn't snag one . . . they promptly added more show dates! 'N Sync harbors a great respect for each and every fan, which is why they don't want even one person to miss a thing.

But even more impressive is the amount of time and *concern* Lance, Justin Timberlake, JC Chasez, Joey Fatone, and Chris Kirkpatrick insist on giving their fans . . . all the time! And though they draw the line at 3 A.M. telephone calls (!!), these fabulous five dudes will go all out in every way for their fans. If that means standing in the pouring rain to sign autographs . . . then so be it. If that means giving out their own, personal E-mail address for a distressed fan . . . consider it done.

So it's no surprise that the guys followed the same rule of thumb when they sat down to plan "The Boys of Summer" tour. Right off the bat each one of these adorable dudes expressed his desire to bring the most awesome show possible to their fans.

**LANCE**'s one wish was to bring you the newest, freshest 'N Sync stuff *pronto!* Knowing that their next CD release wouldn't be until September 1999 — way after "The Boys of Summer" tour. That's why he suggested the group include their newest single from their first CD, "I Drive Myself Crazy," in their stadium shows this summer. Just to give all die-hard fans coming to the concerts a sneak peek into the 'N Sync future!

Dreadlocked dreamer **CHRIS,** self-proclaimed "most playful" of the guys, had some other ideas for this tour. After the last tour, all Chris ever heard were raves about the "sailing stunt." *Did you like doing the sailing stunt? Who thought up the sailing stunt? Are you going to do the sailing stunt* *again?* The questions from fans went on and on, triggering a lightbulb in Chris' adorable head. (In the sailing stunt, the guys are hoisted above the crowd on stage during their rendition of "Sailing.") He also kept hearing how much fans *loved* when the guys squirted them with Super Soakers during the show!

All this attention to the acrobatics got Chris thinking. "Hmmm, we ought to do more stunts!" And even though he does not like heights, Chris was all up for doing even more radical stunts in the summer shows.

**JUSTIN** was headstrong about adding new spice to each tour. Actually, he'd hoped to add something new and different to each individual *show!* But that idea was impractical, seeing as the band would have no time to rehearse something new during their insane touring schedule.

"We want to do something different on every tour," Justin told his fans on-line recently. "A little a cappella . . . a little country . . . a venture into different aspects in the show."

**JC** was *pumped* when it came to getting the plans set for the summer tour. He was diggin' the wild, frenzied musical sets of the previous tour. His wish was to duplicate that energy. "The new tour is going to be amazing!" JC gushed to his fans

4

on-line. "It's going to be huge, different, fast-paced . . . loud! All of the above!" JC was also totally insistent about adding some new remixes to the sets this summer.

**JOEY,** admittedly, has been waiting for this summer tour almost as long as his fans have! For Joey, the whole "party atmosphere" of the tour suits him just fine. "The summer tour will be more just for the music," he announced proudly to fans over the Internet. "FIVE is going to be with us, and Jordan Knight. It's going to be outdoors. Summertime . . . there'll be a lot of partying!"

As for Joey's personal tour touch? What Joey desperately wished for during tour planning was to stay close to the music. "[The arena tour last March, April, and May was] a lot of pyro," Joey told fans. "This tour, we want it to be about our music."

Plainly, with 'N Sync, everything . . . from making important concert decisions to penning the lyrics of a new song . . . is a group effort. A little of this from JC . . . a little of that from Lance. A sprinkle of this from Justin . . . a dash of that from Chris. Add a pinch from Joey, and you have a recipe for sweet success!

# Chapter 2

# For Openers

One disappointment for the guys, in relation to the tour this summer, was an incredible idea they came up with for the show that was nixed by the tour producers. Well, "nixed" may be a little harsh . . . it was more like just too impossible to arrange.

The fantastic idea (and no single 'N Sync guy takes credit for it alone, either), was to get country music superstars Alabama to make a guest appearance at some of the shows. Last May, Alabama recorded the 'N Sync mega-hit, "God Must Have Spent a Little More Time on You," (with the

'N Sync guys singing background vocals). They released it as the first single from their twenty-second country music album, *Twentieth Century,* and it was an instant chart-topper!

The guys had such an awesome time recording with Alabama, they were sure their fans would be hip to a guest appearance by the country legends in their show. Unfortunately, the demanding pace of 'N Sync's summer tour schedule conflicted with Alabama's own touring schedule, so it couldn't be done. But not to worry — it's a safe bet that 'N Sync will still perform the tune anyway on tour . . . at every single show! The sweet song is reportedly each 'N Sync-er's absolute fave.

"The minute we read the lyrics, we knew it could relate to anyone," Justin told his Internet fans. "Actually, it relates to me. I'm a very spiritual person and I think it's the perfect way to tell somebody what he or she means to you . . . if you're really into them."

"It has such universal meaning," Lance keyed in. "It's not just a love song."

Either way, true blue fans of 'N Sync know that to enjoy an 'N Sync show to the fullest, you gotta expect the unexpected. And many would be totally hip to special guest appearances. In fact, all year long

'N Sync fans have been expressing their desire to see the band team up with other pop artists — like Tatiana Ali, Britney Spears, B*Witched, and Janet Jackson, for instance.

The guys, too, would love to hook up with those fine acts on tour. "They're sweet girls," Justin recently told his on-line fans about the girls from B*Witched. "Tatiana's nice, too. Every opening act we've had has been a joy to work with."

But though they remain tight with these talented, dreamy ladies, if they snagged one to open for them this summer, it wouldn't exactly be a *"Boys* of Summer" tour, now would it?

Instead, they're hoping to hook up with some other rockin' fresh talent . . . boy bands in particular. No, you probably won't see the Backstreet Boys sharing the stage with 'N Sync anytime soon (and not because they don't get along, but because they're both major headliners in their own right). But wouldn't you love to see them with: 98°, the Moffatts, or Joey McIntyre.

And how cool would it be if the guys could convince rock legend Phil Collins to take some time from his busy schedule to join the boys onstage for "You'll Be in My Heart," their hit song from the latest Disney movie soundtrack, *Tarzan*.

So pay attention, 'N Sync fans! The show *you* hit this summer might just be the one with that extra, added star sizzle! And hey, if you *don't* happen to catch any special appearances at your 'N Sync show, don't freak out. The boys have made absolutely sure to include tons of superstar power for openers! Adding gorgeous Jordan Knight and his hip-swaying "Give It to You," along with chockful-o'-hunk FIVE's electricity-driven "When the Lights Go Out," makes any 'N Sync show this summer must-see musical magic!

And if you were wondering whose idea it was to have such bodacious opening acts for the tour, wonder no longer. They all worked together to come up with Jordan Knight and FIVE. "We put a bunch of acts on a dartboard," Chris recently joked on-line with his fans. "No . . . :-)" he went on, "Jordan Knight's got a new CD coming out and he's a friend of ours and FIVE we knew over in Europe. So we said, 'Why not?'"

As for that appearance by Alabama? Well, the guys are still keeping their fingers crossed. With 'N Sync, anything's possible!

# Chapter 3

# The Long Days and Nights of the Boys of Summer!

Consider just *part* of 'N Sync's hectic touring schedule this summer: On August 2, they're playing in Indiana. On August 4, it's Tennessee. The next night, Missouri. The next night after that, Illinois. The next night after that, Wisconsin. And the next night, Kansas.

Then a rest, right? Maybe a couple nights to chill with family and good buds? Nope.

The next night it's off to Louisiana, then Texas, then Arizona, then California . . . well, you get the picture! It's one insane summer!

With a crazy schedule like that, it isn't hard

to see why 'N Sync is labeled one of the hardest working groups in the music biz. In fact, by the summer's end, Lance, Chris, Justin, JC, and Joey will have only had a few days r&r. And with their "a-different-state-every-night" itinerary, it's easy to understand why the guys all crack up when they're asked questions like: "What do you like to do in your spare time?" or "Are you dating anyone?"

Spare time? *What* spare time?

In between nightly performances, daily rehearsals, sound checks, set strikes, makeup sessions, costume fittings, eating (McDonalds is a particular favorite), and sleeping, there is little time left for *anything*. Let's face it, when these guys are cruising from city to city on a daily basis, most of their time is spent on a . . . (not very glam!) bus.

And even *then* these guys aren't resting! There's still tons of work to be done: songwriting, some more rehearsing, responding to fan mail, and working out any kinks from that night's show.

Oh, and don't forget . . . *lots* of goofin' around! As you may have caught on their *Mix* home video, they sometimes make up goofy skits for each other on the bus, indulge in massive sugar and candy parties, and play around with a home video camera. "We get loony after a while," Chris admits. "You kind of get used to it," Joey adds. "You pack a lot of clothes, bring a lot of movies and video games. Our bus is our home away from home."

Justin enjoys spending his quiet bus time with a good book. "I have this book I just picked up called *If Life Is a Game, These Are the Rules.* It's a chapter a day and a lesson in life. I like books like that, books that have me ask if I'm doing the right thing for myself."

Joey's complaint about touring is that it's tough to check out the cities you're in when everything's always so rushed. "We have a tour schedule," he said in a recent interview. "And a tour book that tells us where we're going. But sometimes I don't even know where we're going until we get there!"

Some nights, after a particularly pumped show, the guys can't wait to get back to the bus to chill.

"We don't talk, man!" JC revealed on-line. "We *sleep!* We get on the bus and crash. If it's not that, then we're watching TV or videos. Just zoning." (And FYI-BTW, on the bus JC's been known to rest his adorable noggin on a pillow of stuffed animals thrown to him from the audience!)

And what are the videos of choice for this traveling fivesome?

They all agree: *Austin Powers*, the *Godfather* series, and *This Is Spinal Tap*.

As for dating . . . while on tour the guys barely have a sec to see their own moms! It would be quite a feat to keep up a relationship with only a few seconds, literally, a day to spare for a sweet babe.

(Sure, you're thinking: three seconds a day with Lance? *I'll take it!*)

In fact, all five guys have been heard to say that should they suddenly be handed a day off, "catching some shut-eye" is the number one thing they'd be looking to do.

But don't think Justin, JC, Joey, Lance, and Chris are a bunch of tired and cranky campers. On the contrary — they're having the time of their lives! "It's very exhausting," Justin admits to his friends and fans on-line. "But touring is the funnest part about being in the group!"

The others agree wholeheartedly. Actually, JC confesses that the hard work only inspires and energizes them more! "We love the energy and creativity our fans put out during a show, and it makes us work even harder," he said on-line. "The best thing about touring is you get to see the fans. So far our fans have been awesome. I think they must be the most energetic people on the face of the earth."

# Chapter 4

# A Typical Day on Tour

No kidding . . . the guys start *early*. If they're flying, they're up and on the bus to the airport at 4:00 A.M. If not, they usually get started around ten.

First . . . someone walks the dog. The dog?

Yep.

Busta, a pug pup who's been with the group since last March, is the group's mascot. "He's the coolest dog," Chris gushed on-line. "He's got a great personality." The others agree. In fact, there's talk of adding another pooch to the caravan soon!

Next, the guys get dressed. Usually, they have to be decked out and ready for stuff like interviews, press conferences, and photo shoots, so it takes a lot of time getting ready. If they're only headed out for a rehearsal, the guys usually just throw themselves together: T-shirt, jeans, and sneakers. But if cameras and picture-taking is in the itinerary, their routine gets a bit more involved.

Most mornings, Chris is known to take the longest. Mainly because he gets his hair done professionally. As for dressing, that's easier. He just pulls on one of his own funky creations from his cool clothing line, Fu Man Skeeto.

Joey's been known to take a good, long time getting ready in the mornings, too. Some gel for the 'do, a hip-hop cool outfit (probably something black) and, of course, his Superman "J" gold necklace. Top it off with his favorite Nicole Miller cologne and Joey's ready to rumble.

For JC, mornings are a no-brainer: sports shorts underwear . . . and whatever's clean and pressed! (Though he does seem to prefer blue clothes and sporty fashions with stripes.) As for his hair, that takes "about two minutes," he confides.

Justin (whom JC has tagged a total grump in the mornings) is the most particular in the clothes department. He has a certain taste for clothes — mostly Abercrombie & Fitch, and athletic clothes from Champs and Foot Locker. Maybe a Fubu T-shirt . . . a Kangol hat (baby blue to set off his amazing eyes), and baggy jeans. Justin is heavy into sneakers, so it's a good guess that what holds him up most mornings is choosing the perfect pair from his extensive collection!

Lance digs the stripes, too — actually anything athletic. He probably spends the least amount of time getting ready, since his hair (whatever color it is that morning) is pretty simple to control.

After a quick bite, it's off to the venue of that night's concert for a "Meet and Greet" with fans. In the music world, "Meet and Greet" sessions are usually pretty run-of-the-mill: with everything arranged beforehand, the singers pose with the lucky few chosen to meet their idols. The band then signs some autographs, and heads out to chill until showtime.

But make no mistake about it, that's *not* how an 'N Sync "Meet and Greet" goes down! As you already know, there's nothing run-of-the-mill about Justin, Joey, Lance, Chris, and JC. For them, the "Meet and Greet" sessions are the only chances they get to connect with their fans. And if you know 'N Sync they hold their fans in the highest regard.

For this reason, the guys treat every "Meet and Greet" as if it were the most important part of their day. A special time for fans only — all five guys frown upon those prearranged, "We'd-like-you-to-meet-the-president-of-so-and-so's-company" or, "Can-you-autograph-this-napkin-for-the-record-exec's-son's-best-friend?"

That doesn't fly with 'N Sync. For "Meet and Greet," it's true-blue fans only. And the more the merrier! The guys have been known to hand out invites to entire fourth grade classes!

"We've had girls cry and hyperventilate at a 'Meet and Greet,'" Joey reported on-line. "It's wild! Weird. It's a pretty cool scene — we take lots of pictures with our fans."

Justin, too, is bowled over by the reaction of his fans at the "Meet and Greet." "It's funny that people actually ask me for autographs," he reports on-line. "The main thing I want our fans to think about is that we are normal just like them. We like to do things just like them and we go to movies just like them. I find it funny that they get into us as much as they do, but I also find it flattering that they would take the time out to get into our music."

With 'N Sync, "Meet and Greet" can sometimes last for hours. Then, after the last fan has left the venue, and the last morsel of catered grub has been consumed, it's time for a sound check.

At a sound check, the guys walk through their routine along with their band members, and fine tune every mike . . . every electric guitar . . . every synthesizer. At this time, the lighting crew monitors the venue and makes the appropriate light and spotlight adjustments for the guys' show. And don't forget about the special effects! This is also the time to set up any fireworks, smoke, or Super Soakers(!) that will be used during the show.

The sound check usually takes up the rest of the afternoon. Tedious, and sometimes boring sound checks can be the most unfun part of their day! Usually, the guys work straight through dinner, since the last thing they want to do before their high-energy shows is eat!

After the sound check, it's time to get ready for the show. Clothes need to be prepared for a number of costume changes, hair and makeup needs to be done, and, most importantly, those precious vocal cords need to be fine-tuned.

As showtime grows near, each guy gets into his own mindset to prepare for the show. It's a personal thing, Chris explains, since each one has his own individual routine.

"We warm up our vocal cords," Joey explained

on-line. "We warm up our bodies, too. We pray, and go out there and have a good show."

JC's been asked dozens of times if he's nervous before going onstage. "All the time!" he always quips. "Because you never know what you're going to mess up that night!"

Chris even admits to forgetting dance moves on stage! "On 'I Want You Back,'" he confessed in an on-line interview, "I get up there and get so comfortable and stop thinking about being up there that I forget to do a move or something."

In fact, it was Chris who once almost didn't make it on stage for a performance! It was when the guys performed live for ABC-TV's TGIF Friday season premiere. Chris was hanging out in the parking lot with a friend, just chewin' the fat, when he suddenly heard, "Five, four, three . . . " He practically broke the speed barrier dashing across the parking lot to make it onstage. And yes, he made it just in time to hit the first dance move!

Lance admits to "butterflies" before a show. "The first show," he says, "is the most nerve-racking. You never know how you're going to do."

After the vocal exercises, the prayers, the meditations . . . and the hanging out in the parking lot, the guys have one last thing they do before taking the stage. Call it a superstition, but none of the guys will step onto the stage until it's done.

"We never go on stage until we finish a hacky," Justin revealed on-line. "This is a must! It's been that way ever since the first show, first tour!"

"Finishing a hacky" in case you're not hip to the term, is 'N Sync-speak for "finishing a game of hacky sack." And check this out . . . according to Justin, Lance has been known to get way too *serious* about it. "I'm gonna have to talk to him," Justin says with a grin.

From there, (are you ready for this?) the guys embrace in a group hug. (Are you teary yet?) Justin says its just part of who they are — not only guys who work together, but best friends who love and respect one another.

After the hacky and the hug, it's time to line up in the wings and wait for the stadium lights to go down. All five get a surge of adrenaline as the thunderous noise from the audience filters backstage.

The boys are psyched! Pumped like mad! They take their place onstage in the dark. When the spotlights snap on . . . they're ready to rock your world!

And for the next hour and a half, that's exactly what they do.

# Chapter 5

# Here's What You *Do Know*

Pittsburgh, Pennsylvania, native Chris Kirkpatrick founded 'N Sync in August 1995 after recruiting singer and good acquaintance Justin Timberlake (from Memphis, Tennessee), and Brooklyn, New York-born Joey Fatone. Chris knew Justin from auditions around Orlando, Florida, and he knew Joey since they were both working as singers at Universal Studios in Florida. Justin in turn rang his buddy and co-Mouseketeer (from the Disney Channel's *Mickey Mouse Club*), JC Chasez from Bowie, Maryland, and the four guys got hooked up. Chris's vocal coach then put them in touch with Mississippi-native Lance

Bass, who was touring with a Mississippi singing group called Attache.

Their first year together was a major struggle. Every day it was a four-to-five-hour routine for the group. They'd wait for Joey to get off work at around nine, then they'd race over to a nearby warehouse to rehearse.

"We'd rehearse from, like, nine to twelve, or nine to one," JC told *All-Star* magazine. "Straight dancing and singing all night."

It was rough — considering that many of them had already worked a full-time day job! "We didn't take it lightly," JC adds. "We knew what we wanted to do and we concentrated on it. It's not like we got together and practiced for a half hour after dinner. Whenever we had free time . . . that's when we put our energy into it."

With the help of some former *MMC* cameramen, the group put together a promotional video. They also performed at Disney World's Pleasure Island and taped the whole thing. Then they sent out a package of both tapes to dozens of record companies and managers.

The tapes eventually found their way to a German record producer who hooked them up with a record deal in Germany. The same producer

22

had previously helped the Backstreet Boys achieve success in Europe, then in the U.S.

With their harmonious a cappella sound, their electric stage presence, and their extreme talent and good looks, 'N Sync quickly caught fire.

First, there were TV appearances: The Disney Channel . . . *Late Night With David Letterman* . . . *The Tonight Show* . . . *Ricki Lake* . . . MTV. Then they snagged a spot opening for megastar Janet Jackson in October 1998. The fire raged on. . . .

They headlined their own tour a month later, secured a few more TV specials, then celebrated as their singles "I Want You Back" and "Tearin' Up My Heart" soared up the charts. Suddenly, 'N Sync was a hot commodity.

There were more releases, more chart-topping tunes, more appearances (a true fan wouldn't have missed the guys on *Sabrina the Teenage Witch* and *Clueless*!) and a merchandise blitz that would make even Disney characters sit up and take notice!

Another tour in the spring of 1999, then "The Boys of Summer" tour. Along the way they picked up American Music Awards and Nickelodeon Kids Choice Awards. Now Justin, JC, Lance, Chris, and Joey can finally exhale . . . there's no doubt they've made it to the top!

*   *   *

But you knew all that, right?

Okay, then, since you're so in sync with 'N Sync, how about taking the ultimate challenge? You're pretty sure you know it *all*, right? Every last fact?

Good. Then you won't object to a little quiz now, will you? It's pretty simple, really. Just grab a pen, then check out the 100 Bytes You Didn't Know About 'N Sync.

Here's the tricky part: You have to be completely honest, or the 'N Sync-O-Meter won't work! Only a true 'N Sync fan would be totally honest with her answers anyway.

So read each 'N Sync byte in the next chapter. Give yourself a point for each one you already knew. If your 'N Sync-O-Meter adds up to more than 65, you have aced the 'N Sync challenge. Good luck!

And remember . . . no cheating! There's no shame in not knowing a juicy 'N Sync byte. In fact, taking the challenge is a win-win situation. If you know the byte, you get a point. And if you don't know it . . . then you learn something new!

If you're still tempted to cheat, consider what Chris said recently in an on-line interview: "We have the best fans. They're very honest about things."

# Chapter 6

# 100 Bytes You Didn't Know About 'N Sync

**Byte #1**
At the end of "Giddy Up" on the 'N Sync CD, Justin says, "Let's get this crunk!" According to JC, "crunk" means crazy, party vibe, nuts, or wacky.

**Byte #2**
JC made a startling confession recently. He admitted to being the only person in the world who was bored to tears watching the movie *Titanic*.

**Byte #3**
JC dreamed about being a carpenter or an architect before joining 'N Sync.

**Byte #4**

The craziest thing an 'N Sync fan ever did was sneak onto a luggage belt to get past security and meet the boys. Though they don't recommend this AT ALL, they admit it worked!

**Byte #5**

If JC could be anyone else in the world for one whole day, he would choose to be the Invisible Man so he could go everywhere and hear everything!

**Byte #6**

The reason JC is the only 'N Sync-er who doesn't have a tattoo is because he is terrified of needles.

**Byte #7**

During a particularly long airplane trip, the guys pulled a prank on JC. While he was sleeping, they covered him with candy bars and took "incriminating" Polaroids. Then they passed the pix around the plane!

**Byte #8**

JC's first kiss was during a game of kiss tag in first grade, where he received a "soap opera kiss" in the schoolyard!

## Byte #9

Before the group's spring '99 tour they broke the record at the Forum in Los Angeles, California, for the fastest sell-out ever.

## Byte #10

The story behind the group's logo is that while in England, they met famous illusionist/psychic Uri Geller. He told the boys to use a star as an apostrophe in their name on the record and it would be a smash. They did . . . and it was!

## Byte #11

The guys rode the M&M's float in the 1998 Macy's Thanksgiving Day parade.

## Byte #12

The first time the guys heard their song on the radio they threw a party in their van . . . with their stuffed animals (aw!)!

## Byte #13

Some anonymous person cracked up the guys when he cut out pictures of their faces and taped them on babies bodies, then plastered them all over the band's speakers!

**Byte #14**
JC carries a yo-yo around with him everywhere. He keeps it in his backpack.

**Byte #15**
Joey's uncle owns a bakery in Brooklyn. The guys dig the cookies so much, they look forward to all their New York appearances so they can scarf 'em like crazy!

**Byte #16**
Rehearsing for a new tour usually takes the guys a full two weeks of nonstop work.

**Byte #17**
Joey had hoped to be sporting an eyebrow ring this summer, but when he got it pierced, his skin rejected the metal. He also wanted to pierce his tongue, but he doesn't want something that might affect his singing.

**Byte #18**
Joey thinks that if a movie was made of his life, David Schwimmer (Ross from *Friends*) should play him.

## Byte #19

Joey hopes to learn sign language well enough to sign songs during a show.

## Byte #20

When Joey was a little boy he jumped out of a second story window and landed on a mattress just for fun. Needless to say, his parents were pretty peeved!

## Byte #21

One of Joey's most memorable moments was when he met actor Christopher Reeve. An avid *Superman* fan, Joey says he "just stood there and managed to say, 'Hi!'"

## Byte #22

While the guys have never done the spoiled musician thing and gotten kicked out of a hotel, they did once get a warning from a London hotel never to come back because of all the screaming fans camped outside.

## Byte #23

The guys came up with the idea for the video "I Drive Myself Crazy" themselves.

**Byte #24**

The funniest rumor the guys ever heard about themselves was in the *National Enquirer*, when it was reported that talk show hostess Kathie Lee Gifford had a thing for Lance!

**Byte #25**

Chris wears glasses for real.

**Byte #26**

Chris used to be an avid ice skater. Since joining 'N Sync, he doesn't skate anymore for fear of injury.

**Byte #27**

Chris' favorite M&M color is green.

**Byte #28**

The guys usually need two full days to perfect a new dance routine.

**Byte #29**

Chris is a dog person all the way. He says if he ever does break down and get a cat, it's going to be a bobcat!

**Byte #30**
Chris was voted "Most Likely to Be in a Pop Group" back in high school!

**Byte #31**
The guys have each given themselves *South Park* nicknames. Lance is Mr. Hankie, Chris is Cartman, Joey is Kenny, JC is Stan, and Justin is Mr. Mackie.

**Byte #32**
In the third grade, Chris was Tron for Halloween. His mother made the costume for him.

**Byte #33**
All the guys in 'N Sync are mega-Pokémon fans. They were totally psyched to perform the Pokémon rap for a Kids WB spot advertising the cartoon show.

**Byte #34**
The number one question asked the guys is: "How did you guys get together?"

**Byte #35**
Chris got the scar over his left eye when he was lit-

tle, chasing his sister around the house. He ran into a wall.

## Byte #36
Justin and Chris rode Alien Encounter at Disney World together a few years ago, and Chris reports the ride "scared the living jeebies" out of Justin!

## Byte #37
When asked who should play him in a movie about his life, Chris quipped, "Bette Midler."

## Byte #38
Chris recently crashed a motorcycle into some bushes and got plenty hurt — luckily, no permanent damage was done!

## Byte #39
The most memorable gift Chris has ever received from a fan is an autograph from the late martial arts star, Bruce Lee.

## Byte #40
There may be an 'N Sync television series in the works!

**Byte #41**

Chris used to tell people he had a pet tree that he would take for walks and let it "go" on dogs!

**Byte #42**

Chris is the only 'N Sync-er ever to fall out of the bunk bed while the tour bus was moving!

**Byte #43**

Justin's favorite emoticon is :P, because turned on it's side, it's a face sticking out its tongue — something Justin is ALWAYS doing!

**Byte #44**

Once, Justin cooked dinner for a girl. He made fettuccini alfredo with crabmeat and did a great job!

**Byte #45**

Justin's mom takes care of his prized "Benz" when he's on the road. "It's in good hands," he says.

**Byte #46**

Justin is always told how he and actor Ryan Phillippe look like twins.

## Byte #47
The guys work together with their managers to pick the songs they're going to record and perform.

## Byte #48
One of Justin's favorite dance routines to perform in concert is a medley of Jackson 5 tunes.

## Byte #49
Justin secretly wishes Ross and Rachel from *Friends* would get back together!

## Byte #50
Justin's fast food preference is Wendy's over McDonalds. His passion is for the Monterey Chicken Sandwich.

## Byte #51
Justin is way scared of the three S's, as he puts it: snakes, spiders, and sharks.

## Byte #52
Justin's daily workout regimen consists of many, many push-ups. "People don't realize how productive push-ups are," Justin says.

**Byte #53**
Joey got dumped on his very first date! He took her to the movies, and then she dumped him. Joey likes to think it was because the movie wasn't so good.

**Byte #54**
Joey thinks singing a duet with Jewel would be way cool.

**Byte #55**
The best gift Joey has ever received from a fan was a Superman sweater that she had knitted. Joey says it took her two months to make!

**Byte #56**
Once, when Lance was sleeping, Joey put whipped cream on his head.

**Byte #57**
Joey thinks the coolest thing is being at a club and seeing everybody dance and party to 'N Sync songs.

**Byte #58**
Joey loves to use his brother's screen name and

enter an 'N Sync chat room! When he finally admits that it's really him . . . nobody ever believes him!

## Byte #59
To record a single song, the guys usually spend a day or a day and a half in the studio, depending on how intricate the harmonies are.

## Byte #60
Joey's idea of a perfect day is nice weather, and just hanging out all day and talking.

## Byte #61
All the stuff that's tossed on stage during an 'N Sync concert gets loaded onto the guys' tour bus so they can check out each gift after the show.

## Byte #62
Joey never gets tired of eating on the road! He's a huge Mickey D's fan and usually orders either the Double Cheeseburger Meal or the #5, which is the Chicken McNugget Meal.

## Byte #63
The group chooses a single to be released based on which songs get the most votes on their website!

## Byte #64
Lance dyed his hair blue for the Christmas photo shoot last year, but before it turned blue . . . it turned purple!

## Byte #65
Lance's nickname is Scoop because he tends to know the group's schedule before anyone else. He says that usually the guys come to him for news about what's going on!

## Byte #66
Lance's last name is Bass, but ironically it's not pronounced like the musical term, it's pronounced like the fish.

## Byte #67
Lance recently started his own management company. One of his new artists is a country singer named Meredith Edwards.

## Byte #68
The guys' awesome 1999 official tour jackets were designed by Karl Kani. They were first seen by the public when the band showed them to Rosie O'Donnell on her show.

**Byte #69**

Lance wore braces for three years and described the experience as "miserable pain."

**Byte #70**

Lance's first job ever was dressing as a character called Poo Fu! His uncle created the idea for children's television years ago, and Lance played Poo Fu and read books to kids and clowned around.

**Byte #71**

Lance's dream come true was appearing on *The Rosie O'Donnell Show*. "As everyone knows," he explained on-line, "she's like, my favorite person in the world!"

**Byte #72**

Rosie O'Donnell surprised Lance on the show by bringing out actress Lucie Arnaz — Lance's all-time favorite star is the late Lucille Ball, and Lucie is her daughter.

**Byte #73**

Chris has a tattoo on the back of his leg.

**Byte #74**

The strangest thing that's ever happened to Lance onstage was in Europe when a girl in the first row threw water in his face!

**Byte #75**

Originally, Rosie O'Donnell wanted to do a preshow skit with 'N Sync before the Grammys, but unfortunately the music awards show fell on the same day as the guys' first show last spring, so they weren't available.

**Byte #76**

The most romantic thing Lance has ever done was prepare dinner, then take his girlfriend on a picnic to watch the sunset.

**Byte #77**

Lance's first kiss was during a game of Spin the Bottle when he was a lot younger. ("I liked it," he says.)

**Byte #78**

Chris used to sing in coffee shops.

**Byte #79**

The songs "Ginuwine" and "Riddle" were on 'N Sync's European release of their first album . . . but not on the U.S. album.

**Byte #80**

The guys think that the kudos from MTV's *Total Request Live* are the best because it comes directly from the fans!

**Byte #81**

Justin broke his thumb once onstage during a concert! Somebody had put water on the stage and when the guys did a move where they all slid across the stage, Justin went too far and his hand hit the stage and buckled. (Ouch!)

**Byte #82**

Since giving out his E-mail address last year, Chris reports he gets over one hundred letters a day from fans on the Internet!

**Byte #83**

*Entertainment Weekly* photographer Alison Dyer fully expected the guys from 'N Sync to be prima donnas when she had them come in for a photo shoot for the magazine. "But none of them gave me a hard time," she said. "The were some of the easiest musicians I've ever shot!"

## Byte #84
Originally, the guys and Britney Spears were supposed to be photographed in a pyramid for the *Entertainment Weekly* article, but Britney couldn't climb the human pyramid — she'd hurt her knee.

## Byte #85
In the beginning, Joey's mom, Phyllis, took care of the group's fan mail. Just a year ago they were getting four to five buckets a day!

## Byte #86
The episode of *Clueless* that the guys appeared on was called, "None for the Road."

## Byte #87
'N Sync's manager, Johnny Wright, reported in *Teen People,* "I wouldn't dismiss the possibility of 'N Sync and the Backstreet Boys making a record together."

**Byte #88**
JC and Justin once took dance lessons from a former choreographer for Prince and Michael Jackson.

**Byte #89**
The name of the hip-hopper who raps in "U Drive Me Crazy" is Tony Catore . . . who also produced the song "Here We Go."

**Byte #90**
Justin thinks his best feature are his hands.

**Byte #91**
Justin never gets tired of singing the same songs night after night, "Because the songs we sing everyone wants to hear!"

**Byte #92**
Justin bought his mother a princess-cut diamond bracelet last Christmas.

**Byte #93**
Chris loves to sing in the shower. Mostly he practices 'N Sync songs, but some other faves are Busta Rhymes and Brian McKnight.

**Byte #94**

There may very well be an 'N Sync movie in the works.

**Byte #95**

Chris is on record as saying Lance is the klutziest guy in the group.

**Byte #96**

Joey took tap dance and jazz in high school. ("Not very well," he adds, referring to the tap lessons!)

**Byte #97**

Joey says if he could be somebody else for one full day, he would choose actor Robert De Niro, just to see what makes him tick!

**Byte #98**

JC confesses his worst habit is that he procrastinates — to the max.

**Byte #99**

JC isn't always pleased with how his hair looks in pictures! "I think my mom likes the pix better than I do," he said on-line. "I just look and say, 'Oh, that was a bad hair day!' or I'll just cringe and say, 'That's BAD!'"

**Byte #100**
This fall, 'N Sync will be superstar presenters at the MTV Awards, and give a live performance at the Miss Teen USA Pageant.

How'd you do?
Was it a breeze . . . or did you actually learn a thing or two?

Justin, Chris, Lance, JC, and Joey are 'N Sync-able!

Lance Bass

Justin
Timberlake

JC Chasez

Chris
Kirkpatrick

Joey Fatone, Jr.

Lance croons a
concert tune.

Justin connects
with the audience.

'N Sync's killer concerts are always sold out.

A rare day off for the band finds them in cool khakis

The fun factor is huge in FIVE (can you tell?).

FIVE rules the concert stage.

The lad band from Britain tiptoes toward the top.

Abs Breen

Scott Robinson

Sean Conlon

# ROCKIN' yOur WoRLd

# FIVE

BY DEVRA NEWBERGER SPEREGEN

## SCHOLASTIC INC.

New York  Toronto  London  Auckland  Sydney
Mexico City  New Delhi  Hong Kong

Photography credits: 'N Sync cover: Bernhard Kuhmstedt/Retna; FIVE cover: Ilpo Musto/London Features; Page 1: Bernhard Kuhmstedt/Retna; Page 2–3: Ilpo Musto/London Features; Page 4: Anthony Cutajar/London Features; Page 5: Ilpo Musto/London Features; Page 6: Anthony Cutajar/London Features; Page 8 (top): Anthony Cutajar/London Features; Page 8 (bottom): Bernhard Kuhmstedt/Retna; Page 9: Dennis Van Tine/London Features; Page 10 (top): Collin Bell/Retna; Page 10 (bottom): Justin Thomas/All Action; Page 11–15: Anthony Cutajar/London Features; Page 16: Bernhard Kuhmstedt/Retna.

ISBN 0-439-13549-4

12 11 10 9 8 7 6 5 4 3            9/9 0 1 2 3 4/0

Printed in the U.S.A.         40

First Scholastic printing, August 1999

# FIVE

The five guys who are 'N Sync own bragging rights to "hottest boy band in the land."

That's a given.

So's this:

The five babes who are FIVE are the answer to "who's got next?" Step right up and meet Rich, Scott, J, Abs, and Sean — FIVE!

# Chapter 1

# Take FIVE!

Here's a riddle for you (a warning — there's math involved!):

What's 3,000 minus 5?

If you answered 2,995, well, of course you're right! But for die-hard fans of the hit pop music group FIVE, there's yet another answer to the riddle: 3,000 minus 5 equals 2,995 talented young Englishmen who just didn't have what it takes to *be* FIVE!

As the story is often told, back in 1997, a casting call was put out in the United Kingdom for a hot new boy band.

"We wanted something different than the new crop of boy bands," explained RCA Records Marketing Consultant Simon Cowell. "The girl groups around seemed tougher than the boy groups, which didn't seem quite right."

Thus, the "FIVE Project" was launched, after Cowell went on to show the bigwigs at RCA Records that there was a gap in the youth market just crying out for an all-boy band . . . *with an edge*.

England's talented young male population didn't waste a second getting to this particular audition, since Cowell and the RCA guys were the same group of red-hot music producers who'd sent out *another*, similar casting call just two years earlier. Back then, the call was for talented girls to form a pop band. Maybe you've heard of them?

They're called the Spice Girls!

So, with dreams of becoming the Next Big Thing, three thousand English hunks went swarming to the big audition. And from that 3,000, only 14 made the first cut! Then, from the 14, 8 were chosen. Then came another grueling round of auditions, and finally, the final 5 were picked:

**Scott Robinson** from Basildon, Essex; **J Brown** from Cheshire; **Sean Conlon** from

Leeds; **Ritchie Neville** from Birmingham; and **Abs Breen** from Enfield. Five virtual unknowns from different ends of the country, whose backgrounds covered everything from community theater to flipping burgers!

Ironically, each chosen had a teeny "claim to fame" even before hitting it big with FIVE: Oldest member J is a close pal of 911 heartthrob Spike Dawbarn. J even went out with Spike's cousin for four years!

"Spike would stay at my house, and I taught Spike to rap — not that it did much good," J told a newspaper reporter.

Sean grew up in Leeds, literally around the corner from Scary Spice Girl Mel B. "I always thought she was scary even then!" Sean likes to joke.

By now everyone knows Abs is steady in love with girlfriend Danielle Brent, who plays a troubled punk on the British TV show, *Hollyoaks*.

And Scott is a graduate of the famous Sylvia Young Stage School, where he studied with another famous music maker . . . Baby Spice, Emma Bunton.

Almost immediately these five cuties were sent home to pack their things and move into a supercool, three bedroom house in Camberley, Surrey, just outside of London. (Think MTV's *The Real*

*World*!) They were psyched to embark on the unknown, even though it meant leaving their friends and families for the interim. It was the next part that proved to be the most difficult: learning to get along!

"We're tearing you away from your mum and dad and you're going to live with each other and you're going to hate it," record exec Bob Herbert told the guys in the beginning, "but you've got to do it to see if you get on!"

Luckily, in spite of their hugely different tastes in music, television, movies, sports, girls, and, well, *everything*, the guys did "get on." And despite all their differences, Scott, J, Sean, Ritchie, and Abs were able to bond over the one very important thing they had in common: their love for music.

"We hit it off straight away," J told *Big Bopper* magazine. "We all just jelled together."

Scott agrees with his buddy about jelling, though he remembers the scene when they first moved in a bit differently: "It was a complete madhouse!" he revealed to *Seventeen* magazine. "Our neighbors hated us!"

Though the noisy, playful antics of these five new buds may have gotten on the nerves of their new neighbors, living together really bonded their

friendships even tighter. Soon, they were enjoying the same TV shows, sharing some similar tastes in music, and cooking, cleaning, and shopping together.

Not to say everything in the small Surrey home was without mishap. Only a few weeks after moving in to their new place . . . the neighborhood decided they'd had enough and kicked the guys out!

"We had to move five minutes down the road from the old house because we drove the neighbors absolutely bonkers with the noise," J confessed in a newspaper interview. "It's a bit strange because we're five lads who are all really young and it's a neighborhood of middle-aged couples driving Range Rovers. We're trudging up the paths with stereos and stuff like that. They were nervous from the start."

But soon rumors were flying that the guys were asked to leave because of their raucous lifestyle and because of all the girls, girls, girls at their pad at all hours of the night. Stories that Ritchie, Abs, Sean, Scott, and J all flatly deny.

"People made out that fans were camping out in tents on our front lawns . . . even though we hadn't had any success yet! It wasn't true," J insisted. "One article said we were taking girls into the house

**5**

at two in the morning, but there's no way we'd do that. Besides, with the exception of Abs who has a steady girlfriend, we're all single and don't have the energy left for girls after the band work!"

With all that going on *outside* the house, the atmosphere *inside* the house wasn't all hug-hug, smooch-smooch either.

"We were together twenty-four hours a day, seven days a week," Ritchie said in a magazine interview. "So, of course we have our arguments. But they're usually about why you left your dirty socks in the living room."

"At the end of the day," Abs added, "we always knew we were still friends."

Scott summed it up best to an *All Star* magazine reporter. "Obviously, we had our arguments," he said. "We don't try to say, 'Oh, we never argued,' because that would be false. We argued a lot sometimes. Then and now, too. But we know we're friends by the end of the day."

After moving, and bonding, and getting tossed out, then moving again, then fighting, then bonding again, came the hard stuff — the reason they were sharing a pad and going through all this in the first place. Singing lessons, dancing lessons, songwriting . . . composing — there was work to be done!

What the guys remember most about that time, was mainly the uncertainty of it all.

"If someone had told us then where we'd be today," J told *Smash Hits* magazine, "I wouldn't have believed them!"

It was after many long months of endless nights and endless KFC containers, that the guys finally came up with what would soon become their first hit song: "When the Lights Go Out."

"Lights" took off like wildfire and soared straight up the British charts to number one.

And that was just the beginning of a whirlwind chain of events for this brand-new group — events that would launch their careers sky high and transform them into a pop music phenomenon not unlike the funky females before them: Baby, Scary, Ginger, Posh, and Sporty.

But please, whatever you do, don't ever call them the Spice Boys!

"We know the connection is there," Abs told a reporter. "And in the beginning we expected the comparisons. But we're on different ends of the spectrum. We like the Spice Girls and respect what they've done. But we're not about Boy Power."

"Right," Scott insists. "We're about Lad Power!"

# Chapter 2

# High FIVE

The RCA record execs couldn't have made a better call.

Fans today *are* hip for boy bands, especially an electrifying mix like FIVE, with their edgy, on-the-verge-of-naughty style. It's Backstreet Boys meets Beastie Boys. It's a new spice all together: *sweet-boy-Spice*, with some Red Hot Chili Peppers mixed in! And now, after nearly a year since their American debut, not only are British babes clamoring for a piece of FIVE, but coast-to-coast U.S. chicks are diggin' them, too!

This frenzied FIVE fever in the States began back

in November 1998, when word of the group's awesome appearance at the MTV Europe Awards spread like a FIVE-alarm fire! There the guys gave a spectacular rendition of their just-released single, "Everybody Get Up," complete with thirty-five backup dancers! While they sang, everybody *did* get up (how could they help themselves?) to groove with the sassy tune which was, at the time, number one in Europe.

After the performance, FIVE hip-hopped up to the mike to accept the coveted MTV Select Award, whose previous recipients include the Backstreet Boys and the Spice Girls.

But there was no time for celebrating. Though they were ecstatic over the win (the first important win thus far in their short careers), FIVE was whisked away to the airport, heading for the United States. It was time to bring their baby-faced ballads and hip-swaying hip-hop to America.

It was time to dazzle those American girls who were already in love with 'N Sync and the Backstreet Boys with a new blend of edgier, funkier urban dance songs.

When they arrived in the States, to their surprise the number of FIVE fans was already growing. A city-to-city radio tour and some in-store appear-

ances across the country helped spread the FIVE fever, and by April 1999, FIVE was already a major player on the pop music circuit. Teen magazine features, a Disney Channel Concert with Britney Spears, and a huge endorsement deal with Pepsi later . . . and the execs at RCA Records could rest easy.

After two long years, the "FIVE Project" was a major success!

As for their staying power?

Well, even the experts agree the teenage all-boy band market is pretty saturated at the moment. But they also agree that Abs, Sean, Scott, Ritchie, and J have what it takes to rise above the flooded waters and shine! Last fall, the senior entertainment editor of *Teen People* magazine had this to say about FIVE:

"I'm really excited for them. ['When the Lights Go Out'] is so catchy, it's set them up for their next single. But whether or not they have the staying power of the Backstreet Boys, we don't know yet. You have to prove that you're more than five pretty faces."

And boy, have they proved *that*! With one hit single after another, FIVE is making waves all over America! They're one of the most requested bands

on MTV's *Total Request Live* and their songs are among the most requested at radio stations across the country!

Obviously, the fans have spoken.

Now FIVE is making headlines again, this time to the delight of pop music fans all over the country by joining the "Boys of Summer" Tour with 'N Sync! It's a perfect match, too, bringing 'N Sync and FIVE together. FIVE brings to the tour all of the groove, all of the "crunk" that the guys in 'N Sync expect in an opening act. And with concert dates in nearly every major city in the country, there's no doubt summer '99 is a major "Boys Summer"!

It's time to learn more about FIVE! And why kids all over the world are shouting out, "Gimme FIVE!"

# Chapter 3

# Gimme FIVE!

$P$ay a visit to their website www.5ive.co.uk. and it's easy to see why FIVE fans feel their guys are among the most accessible celebs in the music business.

Surf for a while and Sean, Scott, Abs, Ritchie, and J will make you feel right at home. They'll open their world and their lives to you, even asking for your personal feedback from time to time! They'll give you the latest band news and tour itinerary. They'll tell you who had the flu last week, and which of the guys forgot to call Mum. They'll

beg you for E-mail . . . they'll even plead for some photos.

They'll do their best to bring you as close as possible to living the total FIVE experience.

With FIVE you get the real deal. Keep cruisin' their site and you'll see, even with their recent success, the guys are still five normal guys from five normal families from five normal little towns in England.

Scott told *Smash Hits* magazine about one night when he was in the kitchen around midnight eating Coca Pops. He looked over at a picture of him from school and a picture of him from FIVE and realized that everything in his life has changed. ". . . but I didn't think I've changed as a person," he said.

"We're just five guys trying to make something of ourselves," Ritchie explains on-line. "We don't want to be perceived as anything other than a band with wicked songs."

And it's true — they don't have any motivation other than to deliver the finest, freshest most amazing music they can make.

These are good guys.

Really!

They treat their fans well, they support world-

wide charities, and, well, *most of the time* they remember to call their mums!

*HERE'S THE ONE-BY-ONE OF FIVE*

## SEAN CONLON
**Full Name:** Sean Kieran Conlon
**Nickname:** Gungi, or "Mogadon," the name of a sleeping pill! J gave that name to Sean, because "as soon as he sits down, his eyes are closed!"
**Birthday:** May 20, 1981
**Birthplace:** Leeds, England
**Height:** 5' 10"
**Hair Color:** Black
**Eye Color:** Brown
**Family:** Sean has two sisters and two brothers.
**Musical Beginnings:** Sean's been singing since the age of four. He had his first recording session at age eleven and won the Yamaha Young Composer competition at thirteen. The competition was judged by Elton John and Andrew Lloyd Webber.
**Hobbies:** Sean's passionate about rugby, and even considered a sports career at one time. He hasn't played recently, since realizing that "as much as I love rugby, I couldn't sing if I had no teeth."

**Personality:** Shy, quiet, very laid-back. Has a rough time coming out of his shell.

**On Pop Music:** "In England and Europe, pop music hasn't been as [dissed as it is in America]. I think pop music has only recently become acceptable in America."

**Actress He Has a Thing For:** Meg Ryan

**Childhood Hero:** Eddie Murphy

**Sean on Winning:** Sean told *Smash Hits* magazine that winning Best New Tour Act was like reaching a certain level of success. For him, winning more awards this year means FIVE has reached new levels. But he quickly adds that even if FIVE had only won one award, it would still mean a lot.

**Sean on the Success of FIVE:** "I think it's still a shock," he told *Teen Beat* magazine. "We don't take it for granted but we accept it now. We don't think we've gone as far as we can yet. We're trying to get out and get further on. We still have a long way to go yet for us."

**Most Romantic Moment:** Would be somewhere quiet, miles away from noise and people. Sean favors getting to know somebody really well and then becoming close.

**Favorite Music:** Soul and rhythm & blues

**One Thing He'd Change About Himself:**
Sean answers, "Nothing. I don't love myself, but I am proud and happy with the way I am."

## SCOTT ROBINSON
**Full Name:** Scott James Tim Robinson
**Nickname:** Spider (because of his legs) and Curtains (because he used to have long, floppy hair parted in the middle)
**Birthday:** November 22, 1979
**Birthplace:** Basildon, Essex, England
**Height:** 5' 11"
**Hair Color:** Dark brown
**Eye Color:** Blue
**Family:** Two older sisters
**Musical Beginnings:** Scott's been singing since age five and is a graduate of the famous Sylvia Young Stage School.
**Acting Beginnings:** "My eldest sister, Nicola, did quite a bit of acting," Scott told a magazine reporter, "and when I was younger I remember watching her doing all these auditions and wishing I could get up on stage and give it a go, but I was always too shy. Eventually, I went for a show with my sister, and I got the part."
**Previous Jobs:** Acting, and flipping burgers!

**Hobbies:** Music, basketball, and skating

**Actress He Has a Thing For:** Alicia Silverstone

**Scott on Success:** For Scott, winning the Best Male Haircut award was a big deal. His theory is that when girls like FIVE, they'll start voting for them in any awards category — even categories that have nothing to do with music. So when FIVE starts winning "silly stuff" like Best Haircut, it means their fans are really into what they're doing. [*Smash Hits* magazine]

**Scott's Views on the Attention He Gets From Screaming Fans:** "Well, we've been doing this for a while now, and I don't mean this in a big-headed way, but you do get used to it. We've gotten used to seeing the girls, and smiling and waving to them."

**Personality:** "People say I make them laugh. I talk quite a lot, too."


**ABS BREEN**
**Full Name:** Richard Abidin Breen
**Nickname:** Abs
**Birthdate:** June 29, 1979
**Birthplace:** Enfield, England
**Height:** 5' 9"

**Hair Color:** Black

**Eye Color:** Brown, with a touch of green at the bottom

**Musical Beginnings:** Abs has been singing since he was a little boy. "I used to think I was Michael Jackson," he revealed. "I was always around music," he told *All Stars* magazine. "Me and my cousin Izzy, we were trying to start a band when I was around eight! I played the keyboard and we tried to write our own songs!"

**Most Embarrassing Moment:** "When my mum pulled down my trousers and smacked my bum in front of my friends! Oh yeah, I was eight at the time."

**Hobbies:** DJing, music, films, eating out, computer games, and spending time with friends and family

**Actress He Has a Thing For:** Girlfriend Danielle Brent, who plays a punk teen on the British TV show, *Hollyoaks*

**Abs on His Relationship:** Abs knows better than anyone that indeed, "Absence makes the heart grow fonder." It's been rough for him to keep up his relationship with Danielle for the past two years, but he's very committed to making it work. "She

understands my being away all the time," he says, "and she's away a lot, too. It's hard, but I think at the end of the day, everyone needs someone to love."

**Abs on His Hair:** "Every day is a bad hair day," Abs says. "I have mad hair as soon as I wake up in the morning."

**Abs on Success:** "I don't even know how it happened!" he told *Smash Hits* magazine. "Last year, we were the new boys; this year we're headlining and winning awards. I'm like, 'Hold on! What happened in between?'"

**Abs on Music:** Abs loves all kinds of music. "R&B, soul, dance music, everything," he says. "The record company gets us CDs and I've got loads. Plus, when we're in New York, we buy more CDs than you can get in London."

**Abs on the Hardships of Touring:** Sometimes, the guys go for months at a time without seeing their families. It's tough! "I try, every opportunity, if I get a night off, to go home and see my family. We miss so much of our family and friends. It's hard to explain but it's really difficult and that's the worst part."

**Personality:** Abs admits to having big mood

swings and being a bit of a romantic. "I'm really laid-back," he told *Tiger Beat* magazine. "If there's an argument, I just sit back, even if it's a row concerning me! It seems to wind the others up!"

## RITCHIE NEVILLE
**Full Name:** Richard Neville
**Nickname:** Ritchie
**Birthdate:** August 23, 1979
**Birthplace:** Birmingham, England
**Height:** 5' 9"
**Hair Color:** Brown
**Eye Color:** Blue
**Siblings:** One older sister, Tracey, and one older brother, Dave
**Musical Beginnings:** "I came out of my mother's womb singing!" Ritchie likes to say. "I was always singing as a child," he told *All Stars* magazine. "There was a song that went, 'Hands up! Baby, hands up!' and I used to sing that all the time. Then I went to school when I was four and joined the church choir. Then I stopped doing the church thing and I started singing in rock bands."
**Actresses He Has a Thing For:** Michelle Pfeiffer and Cameron Diaz

**Childhood Hero:** Pearl Jam's Eddie Vedder

**Ritchie's Take on FIVE:** "Our stuff's got attitude," he told *Teen* magazine. "It's the kind of music guys aren't embarrassed about listening to."

**Ritchie on Leaving the FIVE Nest:** "I decided to get a place of my own," Ritchie told *Teen*, "because I need my space. I'd like to start dating — I need a nice little bachelor pad. Sean and J are going to move in together, and the rest of us are going to get our own flats."

**Ritchie on Success:** "I dreamt it would happen," he told *Smash Hits* magazine. "My mum always used to say, 'Think big and you'll be big.' We all came into this group with the intention of succeeding and succeeding *big*."

**Ritchie on Life Changes:** Ritchie says he lives a totally different life now than he did before when he was at school, singing in a band with his friends. "We didn't have any serious ambitions," he told *All Stars* magazine. "It was just for fun. Now, I'm traveling the world, working every day. There's not a lot of time off and that's the downside."

**Personality:** Ritchie describes himself as sensitive and caring, open and emotional.

## J BROWN

**Full Name:** Jason Paul Brown
**Nickname:** J
**Birthdate:** June 13, 1976
**Birthplace:** Aldershot, England
**Height:** 5' 11"
**Hair Color:** Brown
**Eye Color:** Blue
**Siblings:** One older sister
**Musical Beginnings:** J has been rapping for years — in his hometown of Warrington he rapped in "Prophets of Da Funk."
**J on Singing:** "Both of my parents are tone-deaf," he says, "so I used to wonder if I was the milkman's son! Then I found out my grandma used to sing."
**Surprise, Surprise:** J is not a fan of the Spice Girls.
**Hobby:** Music
**J on Cleanliness:** "Am I a very tidy person? Oh, yes!" he tells *Smash Hits* magazine. "When I get to a hotel, the first thing I do is put everything away in cupboards 'cause I can't sleep if my bags are lying around the room. Once I've tidied, a bit of ironing chills me out."

**J on House-Hunting:** Since the boys have left the house in Surrey, they've all been looking for new digs. J and Sean are going to be roomies. "We're not sure where it will be yet," J told a magazine reporter, "but I can tell you one thing, it'll have buzzers and security and people won't be able to sleep outside our door!" The reason for that, he says, is because recently a fan kept him awake by ringing his doorbell until four A.M.!

**J on America:** "I like it," he told *All Stars* magazine. "But everything is so different. Everything's bigger [in America] and there's more choice in everything. I like it when I'm there, but after a while I start wanting to get back home."

**J on FIVE's Music:** "We're not just doing ballads with our music," he explained to a reporter, "we add different things, like rap. People have been referring to us as hip-hop and that's a joke. We're a pop band and sometimes we put rap in and sometimes we put hip-hop in."

**Personality:** "Like a true Gemini, I have loads of different sides," J says. "I can be the life and soul of the party, and then the next minute really quiet."

# Chapter 4

# FIVE A-*Live!*

Even back when they were virtual unknowns in the United States, fans lined up just to catch a glimpse of FIVE. In fact, during a Los Angeles, California, record store appearance, the guys were nearly crushed by hundreds of screaming fans! And at the time, they had only released one single, "When the Lights Go Out," in the U.S.

Even the guys in the band were stunned, since they'd only arrived in the country shortly before. "We couldn't tell you why or how it happened that they knew us," J told a newspaper reporter. "But we're not complaining or anything!"

Perhaps it was their baby-faced charm and good looks that caused such a riot.

Or maybe it was because word got out that the same people who brought the world Take That and the Spice Girls were now unleashing another pop sensation.

Or maybe it was because American girls can sniff out a great boy band from a mile away! All that's needed is a few good listens and a tiny taste of a great tune and girls just know.

Or maybe (probably!) the mere charisma of these five lads was so electrifying . . . so magnetic . . . it was just too hard to stay away!

Whatever the reason, since their rise to fame last year with "When the Lights Go Out," and their now ongoing MTV presence with hit videos "Slam Dunk Da Funk" and "It's the Things You Do," the FIVE fan factor has certainly exploded in America.

And truth be told, the guys from FIVE are whole-heartedly grateful. Scott, especially, has only warm words for FIVE's American fans. "They're fine. A bit more polite [than British fans]," he told *All Stars* magazine. "They don't say, 'Get a picture with me!' They say, 'May I get a picture with you?' They're all lovely."

The guys' respect for their American fans is just

another reason to motivate fans to get over to the box office and part with some hard-earned cash. You *do not* want to miss this tour!

"I can never take the smile off my face when I'm in front of an audience," Ritchie said recently in *Teen People*. If you caught the Disney Channel concert on TV, or if you've been groovin' to FIVE's videos on MTV, you know that's true about Ritchie . . . and the other FIVE guys as well. Whether they're rappin' and rollin' with "Slam Dunk Da Funk," or swayin' sweetly to "It's the Things You Do," FIVE's awesome stage presence is really not to be missed.

In FIVE . . . 4 . . . 3 . . . 2 . . . 1!

When the lights come up on stage, Scott, Abs, J, Sean, and Ritchie are ready to rock. It's the part of making music that they love the best: givin' it live to their fans!

"That's always what we've been about," Abs said on-line. "Even when we started up. We couldn't wait till our first tour, taking the music on the road. Just getting on stage with a mike and all these girls . . ."

"The best rush for me is the performing," J told the *Newcastle Chronicle*. "You get such an adren-

aline rush, knowing all the fans are going mad because of what you are doing on stage. The good point about fans," he adds, "is if you are having any doubts about the success continuing, you turn up at places and there are hundreds of girls there."

These days, J and the others aren't having any more doubts of continuing success. They've already conquered the UK, where the number of screaming girls waiting to see them in concert is now in the thousands. And come summer 1999, the guys are expected to get a better taste of their American fans and how the number has multiplied since their last tour last spring.

"It's a shame we can't get around to thank them all personally!" J says about his fans.

You can bet, though, there will be a lot of public thank yous this summer on "The Boys of Summer" tour. With concert dates on a nightly basis in cities across the country, J and the others may very well get the chance to "shout out" all of their heartfelt gratitude to their fans in person!

Of the five, J and band-mate Scott are notorious for taking time out from a set to speak to the audience. As approachable as they are on their official

website, the guys try their best to be as approachable in person. They talk to their fans whenever time permits . . . sometimes even hang out with a group of fans for an afternoon! At FIVE's "Meet and Greet" sessions, the band is always ready with some awesome FIVE merchandise giveaways to give to their fans for free.

What they'll never do is snub a fan, or try to act cooler than cool. "You won't see me or any other member of FIVE walking around with sunglasses on," Abs assures his fans. "We're still the same guys we were before FIVE. And I hardly ever wore sunglasses before, so it's not like I'm into that now."

"With FIVE, we make our own choices," Scott added. "Because we know what teenagers want. At the second audition for FIVE, the guys in the band sort of gravitated towards each other. So the way we see it, we put ourselves together. That's the message we want to get across loud and clear!" And it certainly is loud and clear! On stage and in their music, FIVE goes for mass appeal, hoping to hook the likes of both girls and boys. In fact, they often comment on how they wish they had more boy fans. During their show, the guys try to limit the hip swaying and lovey-dovey, gooey, mushy stuff so as

not to turn away their boy fans. But don't fret —
there's still plenty of love on stage! Especially when
they perform ballads like, "It's the Things You Do."
The way the guys sing "Things," you would swear
their words were meant just for you!

# Chapter 5

# Ten Things You Didn't Know About FIVE!

**News Flash #1: The Trouble Some Will Go To!**

Did you hear the one about the suburban mother of four whose husband LEFT HER because of FIVE?

It's true. Mandy Slater, a thirty-one-year-old woman from South Shields became so obsessed with Abs, Sean, Scott, J, and Ritchie that she spent 4,000 pounds (that's about 6,000 dollars) following them around Britain! The FIVE-crazy mom, whose children range from four to fourteen, has seen the guys perform over one hundred times! "I've slept

out at an airport a few times just to see them for seconds," Mandy reported in a newspaper interview, "and I've waited in the cold and rain to watch them arrive for TV recordings."

Mandy's fourteen-year-old daughter is also nuts for FIVE and goes with her mother to all their shows. And their persistence pays off, too — both mother and daughter get hugs, kisses, and lots of attention from Scott, Ritchie, Abs, Sean, and J, seeing as these are two of their biggest fans!

## News Flash #2: Homesick Ritchie

Feeling the pangs of homesickness ever since taking a place in London — a good distance from his hometown of Birmingham, Ritchie has sought the comfort of another friend — the young, pop-chart-busting Brit, who goes by one name — Billie.

"I met her last summer through my FIVE pal Scott who was at school with her, and she has become a good companion. I don't know many people in London, and she's not from here either," he told a London reporter.

And in case you were wondering just *how close* this companionship is, Ritchie gave it all up when he said, "Romance between me and Billie has blossomed."

## News Flash #3: Beautiful, Bodacious, and *Burglarized*?

Did you know that when the guys first formed FIVE and moved into their humble abode (the first one, before they got booted), four days later they were burglarized?

"We were coming home from a night out at about one A.M.," J told news reporters, "when Rich spotted a shadow in the kitchen. We were all scared, but it was safety in numbers."

As J went on to report, Sean grabbed a shovel and Rich grabbed a rolling pin! (Maybe he was hoping to flatten the guy like a pancake!) Thankfully, the robber heard all the noise and fled. "When we got to the kitchen, we saw the back door swinging open," J said.

Luckily, the thief didn't have time to steal anything valuable from the guys. But still, they all report they were more than just a bit freaked out.

"We have a Sony PlayStation, so we stayed up all night playing it until seven A.M.!" J said. "Nobody dared look at at each other too much in case one of us was caught crying — but we huddled together a bit closer than normal that night!"

## News Flash #4: A Pop Pigsty . . . Squealin' on Sean!

FIVE's hectic schedule keeps them away from home a lot, but perhaps that's a *good* thing. The guys (minus Sean) all report that Sean is the messiest member of the group. They don't even like sharing a hotel room with him while on tour!

"Sean doesn't have the first clue about housework," Rich revealed recently in an interview.

"Our first place was a hovel," he went on. "There were so many dirty plates that we ended up throwing them away and buying new ones! Me and Abs are the tidiest but Sean's so lazy he's in a different class. He's only done about three chores in his whole life!"

J also rags on Sean for being a slob. He tells the story of how one day the guys finally got Sean to do the vacuuming. They were watching TV on the sofa when they heard a strange droning noise. They finally found the vacuum cleaner switched on but not moving. And there was Sean, picking up the dirt and stuffing it under the vacuum!

## News Flash #5: The Half-Past-Three Werewolf of London!

The guys from FIVE certainly have lots to say —

good *and* bad — about one another, and chances are you've heard the dish already. But have you heard the *dis*?

Abs thinks J is bossy.

Scott thinks Ritchie is quiet and shy . . . except when he's snoring, which is most of the time!

Sean thinks Abs is a chat-a-holic.

Ritchie thinks Sean is opinionated.

But the biggest complaint, made by J, is backed up wholeheartedly by the others. J reveals that every day at 3:30 in the afternoon, Scott goes mental!

"He'll be a nice, normal lad all day but something snaps in him and he'll suddenly run around like a lunatic for no good reason!" J told a reporter.

The guys are still trying to determine what freaky force of nature is causing their buddy to have a meltdown every day!

### News Flash #6: He's Not Cellular

Pop star celebs = cellular phones.

A pop star with a cellular phone is just a given, right? But guess what? FIVE's Sean doesn't have one.

While his bandmates are running up their mobile phone bills, Sean remains headstrong about not getting with the cellular program.

"I don't want one until I'm older," he says. "It

makes you too available and sometimes people automatically think you're showing off."

## News Flash #7: Abs the Prankster

You've heard it before from the FIVE guys: Fellow member Abs is by far the biggest practical joker of 'em all! That's why Scott is one hundred percent positive it was Abs who sneaked into his hotel room recently and shuffled CDs, tossed clothing over the lampshades and put ice in the bed — all very "Abs" things to do!

"He swears blind he didn't do it," Scott told a *Smash Hits* magazine reporter. "But because he's always doing stuff like that, I secretly reckon it was him. He's not as sweet as he looks, you know!"

## News Flash #8: Abs and 'N Sync's Justin — Separated at Birth?

Maybe! It's a well known fact that 'N Sync's youngest member has the strange habit of sticking out his tongue. A *lot*. Perhaps it's his way of trying to be "Like Mike" — former basketball superstar Michael Jordan is famous for his tongue-wagging during games.

Or perhaps it's Justin's desire to be "Like Abs"? As fellow FIVE-er J related to *Smash Hits*, Abs'

tongue is almost always exposed! "For some reason," J says, "Abs licks people. He says he's got something wrong with him. His tongue is *always* sticking out! He's only got me once, but if Rich and Scott annoy him, he just runs up to them and licks their faces . . . just like a dog! It's *really* unpleasant."

## News Flash #9: So Suave, Guys!

What makes FIVE different from the other all-boy bands out there? Ask any of the members and they'll say it's their music . . . *and* their attitude. FIVE's music is pop with an edge. And the bad boys of pop will be the first to tell you their whole act is packed solid 'tude.

So how did these calm, cool, and collected singers react when they saw their very first video for "Slam Dunk Da Funk" on TV?

Did they grin oh-so-suave-like, maybe mutter a "Cool, man" or two?

Not quite.

"We were jumping up and down on the sofa and stuff, going, 'I don't believe it! Oh my god!'" Scott revealed to *BOP* magazine recently.

"We were like, 'Who's that? Oh my god!'" Ritchie added. "We were so excited!"

So much for playing it cool, guys!

**News Flash #10: FIVE on the Big Screen?**

Could be!

For the past year, the BBC has been putting together a ten-part POP-umentary on FIVE called *The Big Breakfast*. Chockful of interview clips, behind-the-scenes footage, the guys visits to faraway, exotic places, and *Real World*-style secrets exposed, there's been talk of releasing this video extravaganza on the big screen in the late fall of 1999.

So if you're not able to check out the lads this summer on tour, don't despair! There'll be enough footage and juicy gems in *The Big Breakfast* to satisfy any size FIVE appetite!

# Chapter 6

# Tour Tidbits

Backstage with FIVE is when the pranks fly fast and furious! Particularly back in the hotel room . . . and particularly with Abs as the ringleader! He's notorious for sneaking into his band-mate's hotel rooms and rearranging the furniture!

The others have been known to shake up things at the hotel, too. "J and Ritchie had a food fight at a hotel in Sweden," Scott said on-line, "and got told off by the manager. The rest of us were in the next room trying not to laugh because the manager had come to complain about us dropping water bombs on people from the sixth floor!

Water fights are, in fact, plentiful behind the scenes on tour with FIVE! Reportedly, there's never a show without some backstage water play! You'll almost always find the guys chasing each other around their dressing rooms and throwing water at one another!

How do the guys pass the traveling time while on tour? "Me and Rob [the tour manager] play cards when we're on planes," J told *Smash Hits* magazine. "And I listen to my Discman all the time. It's definitely one of the things I have to have with me." What discs does J chill with? "I've got loads of hip-hop, a bit of soul, and a bit of Iron Maiden. You've got to have the Maiden when you're rockin' out!"

The boys also take cameras with them everywhere. "The camera goes everywhere," J told *Smash Hits,* "to capture all those FIVE moments! I reckon the most embarrassing photo I've taken is Sean's face in the morning, when he first wakes up and he's got no eyes!

"Rich is also camera-mad," J went on, "and he'll snap anything. For instance, we were in the car and he said to me, 'If I get up close and take this picture of your chin with hair on, it might make a really cool abstract picture.'"

At a concert in Australia, the guys had to stop

performing after only the first song because everybody was getting crushed! "It was mad!" Scott remembered in a magazine interview. "They were just grabbing girls and lifting them onto the stage. We were all there dancing and there were all these girls on stage!"

# Chapter 7

# Fast Fact File on FIVE

*The video for "Slam Dunk Da Funk" was shot in an old-fashioned boxing-gym in the Harrow Road. In between takes the guys downed liter after liter of water, since the place was close to sweltering! Blame the special effects department for the temperature surge . . . during the entire shoot, two guys had to hold blowtorches to create a moody haze!

*Abs is most definitely in love (sorry, girls!) with his steady, Danielle. Over and over again he says she's nothing like the troubled punk she plays on

the British soap opera, Hollyoaks. "She's really sweet and is the only girl for me," he gushes.

*"Mum"s always the word where the guys are concerned. In fact, each guy always has something nice to say about his mother in an interview. Scott tells how his mother has saved every article ever written about FIVE, from day one. "She can't stop now! She's spent hundreds of pounds on scrapbooks!"

*The fave FIVE song among the guys is "Everybody Get Up." "It's fantastic!" Abs told *All Stars* magazine. "Whenever we play it — it's our last song usually — everyone, even boys who've been sitting down for three or four songs, gets up as soon as that song comes on."

*Getting along after all this time is still a lot of hard work. "We know each other very well," Abs said in a magazine interview, "but friends argue. We don't get sick of each other, but yes, we get annoyed at each other every now and again. But so do most couples!" "We all have our moments," Ritchie adds. He remembers one argument in particular . . . at the MTV Europe Awards. He and J got into a spat, and the press blew it up out of proportion. In reality there was a little tension between the two during rehearsals, but a little while later everything was fine again.

\*Each member of FIVE has a say in each aspect of their work — sometimes, even the look of their music videos. J remembers how all five objected to a particular scene with flowing fabric that was initially part of their "When the Lights Go Down" video. The fabric was supposed to be all romantic and clingy, but "straight away we said to everybody that we don't do that kind of thing," J said in an interview. "So that got taken out of the script."

\*FIVE's successful single, "It's the Things You Do," was written by Max Martin. That name sound familiar? Well, it should! Max is the same songwriter who brought us 'N Sync's "I Want You Back" and Backstreet Boys' "Everybody (Backstreet's Back)."

\*A Ritchie and Scott Rivalry? At the beginning, when FIVE first started out, Ritchie remembers a bit of rivalry between them. "When we first did radio and we hadn't been in magazines," he told a magazine reporter, "it seemed like I was the most popular member of the band. But once we got in magazines, it was Scott, and he's still the most popular. I don't deny that, and it doesn't bother me. At the end of the day, the more popular Scott is the better it is for FIVE."

\*Songwriting's a group effort for FIVE. Scott explained the process in a magazine interview: "It was

difficult in the beginning because we were all used to writing by ourselves. Everyone was trying to pitch in with ideas, so we ended up deciding on a melody and then all going off to write a verse for it. Then we met up again and decided which bits we liked and which we wanted to get rid of."

Write to FIVE:
c/o Arista Records
6 W. 57th Street
New York, NY 10019

FIVE—They've got next in the boy band battles!
[Top row: J and Rich; bottom, Scott, Sean, Abs]

J Brown